Grandma's Snowflakes

Written by Juli Boaz Karr

ISBN: 978-1-967361-27-4 (sc)
ISBN: 978-1-967361-28-1 (e)

Rev. date: 05/07/2025

Grandma's Snowflakes

By Juli Boaz Karr

Grandma had lived in the same house since she started a family. As the family grew, so did the house.

Four boys grew up in that house, and every winter Grandma would get us out... We are the white vinyl snowflakes that Grandma stuck on all of the windows in the house. "Just in case we don't get real snow," she would always say.

Well, every year we went on display in December and stayed out until Easter. "We still have snow," Grandma would say. Then around Easter Grandma would pack us away until the next winter.

One year, Grandma left one of us out, stuck on the window all year! And oh my! The wonders we were told about when winter rolled around and we were stuck back on the windows. Almost every year Grandma would leave one of us out all year long. The stories were confirmed by those that were left out...

We heard stories of the snow melting and everything turning green. The trees sprouted leaves. Beautiful flowers popped up. There were tulips of every color, daisies, lilies, and purple coneflowers. There were colorful butterflies, ladybugs with spots, bumblebees and honeybees, beetles, June bugs, moths, ants, grasshoppers, and all kinds of bugs. We learned how slug tracks sparkled in the sunshine on the sidewalks. There was a constant chirping coming from the toads and frogs down in Raccoon Creek. And the days grew longer.

We learned about the birds that came to Grandma's feeders. There were robins, chickadees, wrens, blue birds, cardinals,altimore orioles, sparrows, doves, finches, the titmouse, and even hummingbirds with tiny little wings. Sometimes hawks could be seen circling the sky above in search of food.

Nobody needed a coat or hat or mittens. Instead of sledding and snowball fights, the boys were swimming and playing ball. Instead of building snowmen, they were playing in the sand. The boys had swings on a big, old tree. They played in the rain and rode bikes. They held secret meetings in the tree fort. They had outside picnics and fireworks that lit up the sky!

There were no Christmas lights. At night, the fireflies came out and lit up the cornfields and woods. There were storms that lit up the entire sky and thunder that would shake the house.

We learned about the other seasons. In the fall the boys would carve pumpkins and set them on the porch all lit up. Grandma made all of the boys' costumes. There were bunnies, tigers, lions, clowns, bats, and goblins. Children would shout out "Trick or treat!" and get candy! Lots of candy!

At Thanksgiving they all ate turkey with stuffing, mashed potatoes with gravy, squash, corn, green beans, and many breads and pies. Everyone said grace and thanks for all the good food. They all watched football on TV.

We learned what happened during the summer. Who turned a year old? Who started school? Who got hurt? Who learned how to ride a bike? Who had a girlfriend? Who won the homecoming game? Who went to the prom? Who graduated? Who got married? Who had a baby? What happened to the aunties?

The days started to get shorter. The leaves on the trees turned yellow, orange, and red and fell to the ground. The winds grew colder, and once again Grandma would get us out and stick us on the windows. As the snow fell, we would hear all of the stories from the ones that were left out by Grandma. We always listened very well to the stories told... because, after all, it was the family history.

www.ingramcontent.com/pod-product-compliance
Lightning Source LLC
Chambersburg PA
CBHW041146300726
48978CB00016B/1401